RUDYARD THE BUNYIP
and The Magic Swamp

BUDGET BOOKS

ISBN 0 7323 1371 6
First published in Australia by Budget Books Pty. Ltd., 1991
Produced by Mandarin Offset
Story: Tony Johnston
Illustrations: Victoria Nelson
Characters © Johnston / Nelson

Budget Books Pty. Ltd. (Incorporated in Victoria)
MELBOURNE, AUSTRALIA.

Rudyard the Bunyip had to laugh. His friend Hooter the bandicoot was wriggling around in Rudyard's big bulky pouch, complaining yet again about getting his paws wet.

Rudyard's pouch was full of water so that their friend Old Ming the swamp fish could be with them.

"I'm out of here", said Hooter finally, and jumped to the ground.

"What do you want me to do?", asked Old Ming, calling after him, "flap about and choke on the air. A fish needs water."

"Absolutely", agreed Rudyard.

"I'm sorry", said Hooter. "I'm a bit grumpy because it's getting close to the full moon."

Rudyard tipped Old Ming back into the billabong and emptied his pouch. Hooter was shaking his fur dry. He looked like he was dancing a little jig.

Rudyard smiled, then looked up at the pale outline of the moon. He was almost wistful.

Soon, as on every full moon, Rudyard would go into the Magic Swamp, a magical and ever-lasting land for extinct creatures.

It was a Bunyip's duty as guardian of the Magic Swamp, to visit that land on the only days when it touched with the real world — the three days of the full moon.

"Three days is not a long time", said Old Ming to Hooter, "then Rudyard will be back. Why are you grumpy this time?"

"Because one day he might not come back", said Hooter.

"I don't understand", said Old Ming.

"What about when he's the very last Bunyip?", said Hooter.

"Ah ha", said Rudyard interrupting. "But I have some magic of my own. Come, I have a surprise to show you.

Old Ming and Hooter watched excitedly as Rudyard slid into the water of the billabong and swam to his secret place. Rudyard was quite a funny sight as he glided through the water, his small blue dragon-like wings guiding him through the water towards a small nest. Hooter jumped up onto a log, while Old Ming stood out of the water on his tail to get a better view.

Inside the nest were four brightly coloured eggs.

"Bunyip eggs", shouted Old Ming excitedly.

Rudyard swam quickly back across to his friends.

"Shush", he said. "This has to be the biggest secret. Bunyips can only have four eggs every ten years, and unfortunately, when we bunyips have to go into the Magic Swamp we can't take our eggs with us."

"Ah ha", said Old Ming. "Then that's why there aren't many bunyips".

"Because they get stolen", added Hooter quickly.

"Precisely", said Rudyard. "So I want you to guard them while I'm gone."

"Yahoo", shouted Hooter. "More bunyips."

On the first night of the full moon, Rudyard left Old Ming and Hooter guarding the eggs and went to the edge of the swamp. As darkness fell, the moon seemed to increase its power, and like a huge sky magnet it began to drag the murky waters of the swamp upward until everything was covered with a dense and eerie pink mist.

Rudyard smiled as he felt the power of the Magic Swamp reach out for him. It was like he was looking in a mirror at himself smiling and inviting himself in.

And so he stepped through into another world.

The beautiful, glorious, fabulous world of the Magic Swamp!

At the end of the third night of the Full Moon, just before sunrise, Rudyard returned from the Magic Swamp.

He stepped out of the mist as happy as any creature might be after touching the hearts of two worlds.

As always, Old Ming and Hooter were waiting to greet him.

Suddenly, Rudyard's smile on seeing his two friends again disappeared.

"If you're both here", asked Rudyard, "who's guarding the eggs?"

"Hooter twiddled his toes and looked the other way.

"Umm...I..We..", stuttered Old Ming.

"Yes, yes?" asked Rudyard impatiently.

There was a pause, then. "It was horrible...", began Old Ming.

"...then the swamp goanna began gulpng down the eggs", continued Old Ming excitedly, flapping his fins to show how terrified he and Hooter had been.

Rudyard's face was a picture of sadness.

"I could be the last of the Bunyips", he said.

"Ah ha", added Old Ming quickly, "there is SOME good news."

Rudyard's eyes brightened.

"That bully goanna was in such a greedy hurry", said Old Ming smiling, "that he dropped one of the eggs, and..."

"And?", asked Rudyard with new enthusiasm.

"And..I caught it", said Old Ming, mighty proud of himself.

"So where is it?", begged Rudyard, leaping up and down excitedly.

"I swallowed it", said Old Ming.

"I only swallowed the egg to hide it", Old Ming added quickly.
"I didn't eat it."
Rudyard sighed with relief.
"I took it to Lena the mother Brolga for safe keeping. I knew she couldn't have eggs of her own and is always delighted to look after anyone else's eggs."
"And even the swamp goanna is scared of upsetting Lena", added Hooter.
"She has such a sharp beak and short temper", said Old Ming.
"Then let's find Lena", shouted Rudyard.

When they finally found Lena her nest was empty!

This time Rudyard could no longer hold back his tears.

"That's it then", said Rudyard. "Without an egg to come back to next time I won't come back at all".

"But you always told us such wonderful stories about the Magic Swamp", said Old Ming, a little confused. "Why then would you be so unhappy about living in such a wonderful place?"

"Because", said Rudyard, "leaving the real swamp means leaving behind my friends..."

During the next few weeks Rudyard was comforted by Old Ming and Hooter. Even Bluey Wombat dug what seemed like hundreds of holes around the edges of the swamp, looking for the eggs in the hope that Lena had hidden them. But no luck.

Old Ming and Hooter tried very hard to come to terms with the tragedy of the lost bunyip egg. When the next Full Moon finally approached, Old Ming and Hooter knew the time was fast approaching for Rudyard to leave.

On the final night Rudyard let out such a sad and soulful howl that all the creatures of the swamp wept for his unhappiness.

"The last of the bunyips", croaked Hooter sadly as Rudyard moved forward. Then he and Old Ming watched Rudyard head into the pink mist of the Magic Swamp.

To Rudyard's surprise the first thing he saw inside the Magic Swamp was Lena the Brolga.

"I've been so excited", she screeched. "I didn't think I'd be able to last until the Full Moon came around. Wonderful news. wonderful news", she chattered away.

Rudyard was equally as excited.

"I was the last of the Southern Brolgas", explained Lena.

"I had no warning, no time to prepare, no time to tell Old Ming. The last of the mist simply swallowed me up, the nest and the eggs. Suddenly I was here."

"You were in the Magic Swamp all this time?", asked Rudyard.

"We were", corrected Lena, smiling.

"Meet the littlest bunyip", screeched Lena excitedly as she flapped her wings and rose up from the nest to reveal — three baby orphan birds and...Rudyard's new baby bunyip!

"You know what this means?" shouted Rudyard up to Lena.

"You can go back to your friends", she replied.

Word spread quickly from the edges of the swamp to the far side of the billabong. On the third day of the full moon Rudyard had returned through the mist.

Hooter who had been brooding by the possum tree, hugged Rudyard and then raced off to tell Old Ming and Bluey so that before long a welcoming party had gathered.

"Look", said Rudyard to his friends, "I have a surprise."